Frederick George Scott

The Unnamed Lake

And other Poems

Frederick George Scott

The Unnamed Lake
And other Poems

ISBN/EAN: 9783744722483

Printed in Europe, USA, Canada, Australia, Japan

Cover: Foto ©Andreas Hilbeck / pixelio.de

More available books at **www.hansebooks.com**

THE UNNAMED LAKE

And Other Poems

BY

FREDERICK GEORGE SCOTT

AUTHOR OF "THE SOUL'S QUEST," "MY LATTICE," ETC.

TORONTO:
WILLIAM BRIGGS
WESLEY BUILDINGS.

———

MDCCCXCVII.

CONTENTS.

		PAGE
THE UNNAMED LAKE		7
A DREAM OF THE PREHISTORIC		10
EOTHEN		15
A REVERIE		16
SONG'S ETERNITY		19
LOST LOVE		20
BURIED LOVE		22
TO A FLY IN WINTER		24
SUNRISE		27
AMONG THE SPRUCES		29
THE EXCEEDING BITTER CRY		31
AT THE CROSS ROADS		33
A SONG OF TRIUMPH		35

SONNETS.

	PAGE
TO THE SEA	42
ISCARIOT	43
MANHOOD	44
THE HEAVEN OF LOVE	45
LOVE'S ETERNITY	46
AT NIGHTFALL	47
EASTER ISLAND	48

THE UNNAMED LAKE.

THE UNNAMED LAKE.

It sleeps among the thousand hills
　　Where no man ever trod,
And only nature's music fills
　　The silences of God.

Great mountains tower above its shore,
　　Green rushes fringe its brim,
And o'er its breast for evermore
　　The wanton breezes skim.

Dark clouds that intercept the sun
　　Go there in Spring to weep,
And there, when Autumn days are done,
　　White mists lie down to sleep.

Sunrise and sunset crown with gold
  The peaks of ageless stone,
Where winds have thundered from of old
  And storms have set their throne.

No echoes of the world afar
  Disturb it night or day,
But sun and shadow, moon and star,
  Pass and repass for aye.

'Twas in the grey of early dawn,
  When first the lake we spied,
And fragments of a cloud were drawn
  Half down the mountain side.

Along the shore a heron flew,
  And from a speck on high,
That hovered in the deepening blue,
  We heard the fish-hawk's cry.

Among the cloud-capt solitudes,
  No sound the silence broke,
Save when, in whispers down the woods,
  The guardian mountains spoke.

Through tangled brush and dewy brake,
  Returning whence we came,
We passed in silence, and the lake
  We left without a name.

A DREAM OF THE PREHISTORIC.

NAKED and shaggy, they herded at eve by the sound
of the seas,
When the sky and the ocean were red as with
blood from the battles of God,
And the wind like a monster sped forth with its feet
on the rocks and the trees,
And the sands of the desert blew over the wastes
of the drought-smitten sod.

Here, mad with the torments of hunger, despairing
they sank to their rest,
Some crouching alone in their anguish, some
gathered in groups on the beach ;
And with tears almost human the mother looked
down at the babe on her breast ;
And her pain was the germ of our love, and her
cry was the root of our speech.

Then a cloud from the sunset arose, like a cormorant
    gorged with its prey,
  And extended its wings on the sky till it smothered
    the stars in its gloom,
And ever the famine-worn faces were wet with the
    wind-carried spray,
  And dimly the voice of the deep to their ears was
    a portent of doom.

And the dawn that rose up on the morrow, apparelled
    in gold like a priest,
  Through the smoke of the incense of morning,
    looked down on a vision of death ;
For the vultures were gathered together and circled
    with joy to their feast
  On hearts that had ceased from their sorrow, and
    lips that had yielded their breath.

Then the ages went by like a dream, and the shore-
    line emerged from the deep,
  And the stars as they watched through the years
    saw a change on the face of the earth ;

For over the blanket of sand that had covered the
    dead in their sleep
  Great forests grew up with their green, and the
    sources of rivers had birth.

And here in the after-times, man, the white-faced and
    smooth-handed, came by,
  And he built him a city to dwell in and temples of
    prayer to his God;
He filled it with music and beauty, his spirit aspired
    to the sky,
  While the dead by whose pain it was fashioned lay
    under the ground that he trod.

He wrenched from great Nature her secrets, the
    stars in their courses he named;
  He weighed them and measured their orbits, he
    harnessed the horses of steam;
He captured the lightnings of heaven, the waves of
    the ocean he tamed,—
  And ever the wonder amazed him as one that
    awakes from a dream.

But under the streets and the markets, the banks
and the temples of prayer,
Where humanity laboured and plotted, or loved
with an instinct divine,
Deep down in the silence and gloom of the earth
that had shrouded them there
Were the fossil remains of a skull and the bones of
what once was a spine.

Enfolded in darkness forever, untouched by the
changes above,
And mingled as clay with the clay which the
hands of the ages had brought,
Were the hearts in whose furnace of anguish was
smelted the gold of our love,
And the brains from whose twilight of instinct has
risen the dawn of our thought.

But the law, that was victor of old with its heel on
the neck of the brute,
Still tramples our hearts in the darkness, still grinds
down our face in the dust;

We are sown in corruption and anguish—whose
  fingers will gather the fruit ?
  Our life is but lent for a season—for whom do we
    hold it in trust ?

In the vault of the sky overhead, in the gulfs that lie
  under our feet,
  The wheels of the universe turn and the laws of
    the universe blend ;
The pulse of our life is in tune with the rhythm of
  forces that beat
  In the surf of the furthest star's sea, and are spent
    and regathered to spend.

Yet we trust in the will of the Being whose fingers
  have spangled the night
  With the dust of a myriad worlds, and who speaks
    in the thunders of space ;
Though we see not the start or the finish, though
  vainly we cry for the light,
  Let us mount in the glory of manhood and meet
    the God-Man face to face.

EOTHEN.

The immortal spirit hath no bars
  To circumscribe its dwelling place ;
My soul hath pastured with the stars
  Upon the meadow-lands of space.

My mind and ear at times have caught,
  From realms beyond our mortal reach,
The utterance of Eternal Thought,
  Of which all nature is the speech.

And high above the seas and lands,
  On peaks just tipped with morning light,
My dauntless spirit mutely stands
  With eagle wings outspread for flight.

A REVERIE.

O TENDER love of long ago,
   O buried love, so near me still
On tides of thought that ebb and flow,
   Beyond the empire of the will ;
To-night with mingled joy and pain
I fold thee to my heart again.

And down the meadows, dear, we stray,
   And under woods still clothed in green,
Though many Springs have passed away
   And many harvests there have been,
Since through the youth-enchanted land
We wandered idly hand in hand.

Then every brook was loud with song,
   And every tree was stirred with love,
And every breeze that passed along
   Was like the breath of God above ;—

And now to-night we go the ways
We went in those sweet summer days.

Dear love, thy dark and earnest eyes
   Look up as tender as of yore,
And, purer than the evening skies,
   Thy cheeks have still the rose they wore ;
I—I have changed but thou art fair
And fresh as in life's morning air.

What little hands these were to chain
   So many years a wayward heart ;
How slight a girlish form to reign
   As queen upon a throne apart,
In a man's thought, through hopes and fears,
And all the changes of the years.

Dear girl, behold, thy boy is now
   A man and grown to middle age,
The lines are deep upon his brow,
   His heart hath been grief's hermitage ;
But hidden where no eye can see
His boyhood's love still lives for thee,—

Still blooms above thy grave to-day,
   Where death hath harvested the land,
Though such long years have passed away
   Since down the meadows hand in hand
We went with hearts too full to know
How deep their love was long ago.

SONG'S ETERNITY.

LITTLE bird on dewy wing
    In the dawn of day,
All the pretty songs you sing
    Pass away.
For although man's heart is stirred
    By your happy voice,
You can only sing one word,—
    " Rejoice," " Rejoice."

But the music poets make
    Is a deathless strain,
For they do from sorrow take,
    And from pain,
Such a sweetness as imparts
    Joy that never dies,—
And their songs live in men's hearts
    Beyond the skies.

LOST LOVE.

LOVE has gone a-straying,
   Like a cloud in May,
Down the silent wind-ways,
   Past the bounds of day.
When will he return again ?
When will his fire burn again ?
   I am broken-hearted,
   Since sweet Love departed.

Love has gone a-straying—
   Call him back to me,
Up the silent wind-ways,
   Over land and sea.
Tell him he must bring again
Joys that I can sing again ;
   I am broken-hearted,
   Since sweet Love departed.

Love has gone a-straying—
  Foolish, foolish Love,
Seeking up the wind-ways
  For the stars above ;
Tell him here are flowers as fair,
Tell him here are hours as rare,
While the earth is dressed in spring
And the merry birds do sing,
And the brooks and rivers run
Laughing at the staid old sun ;
Call Love home again,
Bid him not roam again,—
  I am broken-hearted,
  Since sweet Love departed.

BURIED LOVE.

LOVE hath built himself a house
   Underneath the snow,
Where, amid the winter's storm,
He can keep his body warm,
   When the winds do blow.

It is lined with leaves that fell
   Half a year ago,
And around it linger yet
Odours of spring violet,
   Underneath the snow.

If you come and try to peep
   Into what's below,
Laughing loud, as if in fun,
Love jumps up and makes you run,
   Pelting you with snow.

What does Love do night and day?
Would you like to know?
In the dark he sits and weeps
For a little maid that sleeps—
Sleeps beneath the snow.

And when spring shall come again
And the warm winds blow,
Tears have made his sight so dim
That the world will seem to him
Buried still in snow.

TO A FLY IN WINTER.

Good day, little Fly,
Here we are—you and I,
    The children of summer ;
Warm your wings at the fire,
Take what food you desire,
Your Lordship I'll hire
    As my fifer and drummer.

Outside the winds blow,
And the fast falling snow
    From the gables is drifting ;
The clouds seem to me
Like an overturned sea
Lashing field, fence and tree,
    Never breaking or lifting.

Tune up, little Friend,
Tell me winter will end,
 And the spring-time is coming ;
When the buds with surprise
Will rub their young eyes
And look up to the skies,
 At thy fifing and drumming.

Sing me carols of May,
And of June and the hay,
 With the sweet-smelling clover ;
Of the soft winds that creep
Round my bed as I sleep,
When the dawn lights the deep,
 And the long night is over.

Sing me songs of the brook
Where the little fish look
 Up, with eyes full of wonder,
At the wind-shaken screen
Of the willows that lean
Over pools that are green
 As the boughs they sleep under.

Tune up, little Friend,
For the winter will end,—
    Be my fifer and drummer;
And thy one song repeat,
Till its buzz and the heat
Give my dreaming the sweet
    Taste of meadows and summer.

SUNRISE.

O RISING Sun, so fair and gay,
What are you bringing me, I pray,
Of sorrow or of joy to-day ?

You look as if you meant to please,
Reclining in your gorgeous ease
Behind the bare-branched apple-trees.

The world is rich and bright, as though
The pillows where your head is low
Had lit the fields of driven snow.

The hoar-frost on the window turns
Into a wood of giant ferns
Where some great conflagration burns.

And all my childhood comes again
As lightsome and as free from stain
As those frost-pictures on the pane.

I would that I could mount on high
And meet you, Sun—that you and I
Had to ourselves the whole wide sky.

But here my poor soul has to stay,
So tell me, rising Sun, I pray,
What are you bringing me to-day?

What shall this busy brain have thought;
What shall these hands and feet have wrought;
What sorrows shall the hours have brought,

Before thy brilliant course is run,
Before this new-born day is done,
Before you set, O rising Sun?

AMONG THE SPRUCES.

'Tis sweet, O God, to steal away,
  Before the morning sun is high,
Upon some frosty winter's day,
  When not a cloud is on the sky,
And all the world is white below,
Knee-deep with freshly fallen snow,—

To steal into the silent woods
  Before the trees are quite awake,
And watch them in their snowy hoods
  A rough-and-ready toilet make,
When in the little breezes creep
And rouse them gently from their sleep.

'Tis sweet, O God, to kneel among
  The snow-bent trees, and lift the mind
Above the boughs where birds have sung,
  Above the pathways of the wind,

Into the very heart of space,—
To where the angels see Thy face.

And as my spirit mounts in prayer,
  So keen becomes its mystic sight,
That through the sunshine in the air
  I see a new and heavenly light,
And all the bowed woods seem to be
Acknowledging the Trinity.

THE EXCEEDING BITTER CRY.

JANUARY, 1897.

FROM the lands burnt dead with sunshine, where our
    fathers fought and bled,
And have reaped a golden harvest, comes a cry to us
    for bread ;
For the millions, famine-stricken, starve and sicken
    in despair,
And the glazing eyes of famine see the vultures in
    the air.

Shall we shut up human pity ? Shall they cry to
    us in vain ?
Shall we sate ourselves with plenty, while they
    perish in their pain ?
Can we kneel and say " Our Father,"—can our spirits
    hope for rest,
While the babe lies dead from starving on its starving
    mother's breast ?

They are black,—but they are brothers, and they
    suffer pain as we,
And the four great winds of heaven bring their death-
    cries o'er the sea ;
They are black,—but they are brothers, and the flag
    of England stands
Where the dead forms, drawn together, dry and
    whiten on the sands.

Lion-blooded sons of England, breathing glory as
    your breath,
Up and gird you now, my brothers, for a giant strife
    with death ;
By the flag we guard unsullied, by the God that
    reigns above,
Rise and bind our mighty empire with the bands of
    human love.

AT THE CROSS ROADS.

HERE on life's Cross Roads, friend, our ways now
    sever,
  And each must journey 'neath an altered sky,
Yet in the years to come our hearts will never
  Forget the glad hours of the days gone by.

Oft have we sat before the bright logs blazing
  On the wide hearth, and closed the winter's day ;
Oft in the meadows, where the cows were grazing,
  Have watched the summer sunsets die away.

Oft have we sped, girt with the engine's thunder,
  Down the bright track into the golden dawn ;
Oft through dark forests when the moon, in wonder,
  Peered 'neath the trees at the long smoke out-
    drawn.

And now when autumn fields are filled with beauty,
　　And while the breath of harvest is so sweet,
We who have heard afar the voice of duty,
　　Shake hands and part where these two roadways
　　　meet.

Dear brother heart, we leave farewells unspoken,
　　We shall not change nor can our love forget,
For on life's sky, by sun and shadow broken,
　　True friendship is a star that does not set.

A SONG OF TRIUMPH.

Ye tempests that sweep o'er the deep, heavy-browed
    with the cloud of the rain,
Assemble in wonder with thunder and bellowing
    voice of the main,
With the roar that comes forth from the North when
    the ice-peaks roll down to the sea,
And the dream of the gleaming white silence is
    hoarse with waves' laughter and glee ;—
Yea, gather, ye tempests, on wings, with the strings
    of God's harp in your hands,
And your voices upraise in the praise of the Lord of
    the seas and the lands.

Sing the triumph of Man, who began in the caves
    where the waves lay asleep,
In a cradle made green by the sheen of the sunlight
    that smote on the deep,

When the ages. were young and the tongue of the
 universe sounded its praise,
Over the dismal, abysmal, dark voids where God
 went on His ways
To crown His creations with nations of flowering and
 animate life :—
Implanting a germ in the worm that would grow to
 His image through strife.

The jungles that spread on the bed of the plain,
 where the rain and the snow
Came down from the mountains a river, to shiver in
 torrents below,
Were alight with the bright coloured snakes and the
 tigers that lurked for their prey,
While the bird that was heard in the boughs had a
 plumage more splendid than day,
But the lord at whose word all were humbled was
 Man who in majesty came ;—
Immortal as God and who trod with his body erect
 as a flame.

Let the praise of Man's form by the storm be
  outrolled to the gold of the West,
To the edge of the ledge of the clouds where the sun
  marches down to his rest.
For out of the rout of fierce famine, of warfare and
  hunger and strain,
Man's body was fashioned and passioned in frenzy of
  fury and pain.
He goes with his face upon space, like a god he is
  girded with might,
His desire is the fire of a star that illumines a
  limitless night.

His love is above and beneath him, a mountain and
  fountain of fire,
In his blood is the flood of the tiger and claws of its
  hate and desire ;
In his thought is the speed of the steed as it courses
  untrammelled and free,
With its sinews astrain on the plain where the winds
  are as wide as the sea ;
But his soul is the roll of the ocean that murmurs in
  darkness and day,
A part of the heart of creation that lives while the
  ages decay.

3

It mounts upon wings through the rings of the night
    that is bright with the stars,   .

Till at length in its strength it has broken the chains
    of the flesh and its bars,

And waits for the hush and the flush of the dawn of
    which God is the sun ;—

The dawn that will rise in the skies when the night
    of our warfare is done ;

When Man shall behold, in the gold of the firmament
    passing in heat,

The face of the Proved and Beloved who descends
    with the stars at His feet.

Then the past shall be cast like the sand that a hand
    may throw out to the sea,

Shall be cast out of sight into night, and our man-
    hood, resplendent and free,

Shall wander in dreams by the streams where the
    waters are silent as sleep,

Or winged on God's errands shall soar through the
    roar of the fathomless deep,

When the lightning is brightening our course and the
    thunder-clouds roll in our face,—

For the soul that is pure shall endure when the
    planets have crumbled in space.

Ye tempests that sweep from the deep which the
night and the light overspan,

Assemble in splendour and render the praise of
magnificent Man ;

In his hands are the sands of the ages, and gold of
unperishing youth,

On his brow, even now, is the shining of wisdom and
justice and truth ;

His dower was the power to prevail, on the lion and
dragon he trod,

His birth was of earth but he mounts to a throne in
the bosom of God.

SONNETS.

TO THE SEA.

O STRANGE, sublime, illimitable Sea,
   Majestic in thy sovran self-control,
   And awful with the furious tides that roll
Round Earth's proud cliffs who bow their heads to
       thee ;—
Thou art like God in thy vast liberty,
   Thy throne is the wide world from pole to pole,
   Thy thunders are Time's passing bell, and toll
The knell of all that has been, is, and is to be.

O mighty rock-bound Spirit, bright to-day,
   To-morrow leaden 'neath the clouds of gloom,
   Or mystic with the stars that overspan,—
Beneath thy billows, where the wild winds play,
   There broods a darkness deeper than the tomb,
   In caverns voiceless since the world began.

ISCARIOT.

MEEK, passionless, precise, with pallid face,
   Judas grew up, his mother's constant joy,
   Who thanked Jehovah daily that her boy
Of boyhood's viciousness had not a trace.
Yet, in the heart of that which she thought grace,
   A devil lurked more subtle to destroy
   Than any other Satan doth employ
To wreak his vengeance on the human race.

In after years the man's soul grew so dead,
   That when he met Love's Self and held Love's
      Hand,
   Nay, kissed Love's Lips, he still could Love with-
      stand.
Too late, the thirst which drove him to his doom
   Was quenched, when back the abhorrent daylight
      fled
From that lone gibbet darkening in the gloom.

MANHOOD.

WITH child-faith dead, and youth-dreams gone like
    mist,
  We stand, at noon, beneath the blazing sun
  Upon life's dusty road, our course half done.
No more we stray through woods where birds hold
    tryst,
Nor over mountains which the dawn hath kissed;
  In glare and heat the race must now be run
  On this blank plain, while round us, one by one,
Our friends drop out and urge us to desist.

Then from the brazen sky rings out a voice,
"Faint not, strong souls, quit you like men, rejoice,
That now like men ye bear the stress and strain,
  With eyes unbound seeing life's naked truth.
Gird up your loins, press on with might and main,
  And taste a richer wine than that of youth."

THE HEAVEN OF LOVE.

I ROSE at midnight and beheld the sky
   Sown thick with stars, like grains of golden sand
   Which God had scattered loosely from His hand
Upon the floorways of His house on high ;
And straight I pictured to my spirit's eye
   The giant worlds, their course by wisdom planned,
   The weary wastes, the gulfs no sight hath spanned,
And endless time for ever passing by.

Then, filled with wonder and a secret dread,
   I crept to where my child lay fast asleep,
With chubby arm beneath his golden head.
What cared I then for all the stars above ?
   One little face shut out the boundless deep,
One little heart revealed the heaven of love.

LOVE'S ETERNITY.

BETWEEN the stars, the light-waves on and on
   Roll from the scenes of earth's past history
   Unto the margins of eternity.
No day is lost of all that ever shone,
Each with its story into space hath gone
   So that, to-night, some distant world may see,
   Looking at earth, the Cross on Calvary,
Or the green plain and camps at Marathon.

Dear heart, whose life is woven into mine,
   Who art the light and music of my days,
     We move towards death, yet let us have no
      fear ;
   If nothing dies, not even light's faintest rays,
Sure that vast love which links my soul with thine
     Marks for eternity our union here.

AT NIGHTFALL.

O LITTLE hands, long vanished in the night—
   Sweet fairy hands that were my treasure here—
   My heart is full of music from some sphere,
Where ye make melody for God's delight.
Though autumn clouds obscure the starry height,
   And winds are noisy and the land is drear,
   In this blank room I feel my lost love near,
And hear you playing,—hands so small and white.

The shadowy organ sings its songs again,
   The dead years turn to music at its voice,
     And all the dreams come back my brain did
     store.
Once more, dear hands, ye soothe me in my pain,
   Once more your music makes my heart rejoice,—
   God speed the day we clasp for evermore!

EASTER ISLAND.

THERE lies a lone isle in the tropic seas,—
   A mountain isle, with beaches shining white,
   Where soft stars smile upon its sleep by night,
And every noon-day fans it with a breeze.
Here on a cliff, carved upward from the knees,
   Three uncouth statues of gigantic height,
   Upon whose brows the circling sea-birds light,
Stare out to ocean, over the tall trees.

Forever gaze they at the sea and sky,
   Forever hear the thunder of the main,
    Forever watch the ages die away;
And ever round them rings the phantom cry
   Of some lost race that died in human pain,
    Looking towards heaven, yet seeing no more
    than they.